MERMAID

(OR, HOW TO FIND LOVE UNDERWATER)

Thank you, Bayla Braun: the original Princess-Fish.

And for my daughter, Lucy Ava, still swimming deep inside me while I finished this book:
I waited my whole life to be your mother—I love you past the end of the ocean.
—J.M.F.

To my daughter, Juniper.
—G.T.

Text ~~The Little~~ Mermaid (Or, How to Fall in Love Underwater) © 2021 J.M. Farkas
Illustrations copyright © 2021 Gina Triplett

This version of "The Little Mermaid," by Hans Christian Andersen, translated by M. R. James,
was originally published in *Forty-Two Stories*, by Faber & Faber Ltd., London (1930).

Book design by Melissa Nelson Greenberg

Library of Congress Cataloging-in-Publication Data available
ISBN: 978-1-951836-07-8

Printed in China

10 9 8 7 6 5 4 3 2 1

Cameron Kids is an imprint of Cameron + Company

Cameron + Company
Petaluma, California
www.cameronbooks.com

~~THE LITTLE~~ MERMAID
(OR, HOW TO FIND LOVE UNDERWATER)

A BLACKOUT POEM
BY ~~HANS CHRISTIAN ANDERSEN~~ J. M. FARKAS

ILLUSTRATED BY GINA TRIPLETT

cameron kids

Far out in the sea the water is as blue as the petals of the loveliest of cornflowers, and as clear as the clearest glass; but it is very deep, deeper than any anchor-cable can reach, and many church towers would have to be put one on the top of another to reach from the bottom out of the water. Down there live the sea people.

Now you must not think for a moment that there is only a bare white sandy bottom there; no, no, there the most extraordinary trees and plants grow, which have stems and leaves so supple that they stir at the slightest movement of the water, as if they were alive. All the fish, big and little, flit among the branches, like the birds in the air up here. In the deepest place of all lies the sea king's palace. The walls are of coral and the tall pointed windows of the clearest possible amber, but the roof is of mussel-shells that open and shut themselves as the water moves. It all looks beautiful, for in everyone of them lie shining pearls, a single one of which would be the principal ornament in a Queen's crown.

The sea King down there had been a widower for many years, but his old mother kept house for him. She was a clever woman, but

proud of her rank, for which reason she went
about with twelve oysters on her tail, while
the rest of the nobility might only carry six.
For the rest she deserved high praise, espe-
cially because she was so fond of the little sea
Princesses, her grandchildren. There were six
of them, beautiful ch   the youngest
was the prettiest o   kin was as
           nd pure

                                             play

                                              ch
   m   th   th   al-
   ys fl in   indo   ut
        o   to th le
  rinc   fe   nds a   l-
low t   elv s t

   O   de   larg   r
den wi fiery   ees, w
fruit   e li   owers we
like a fla nin   were always
moving thei   The ground
was of the fir   ike the ame
of sulphur. C   xpanse down

2

there lay a wonderful blue sheen. You could more easily imagine that you were far up in the air and could see the sky above you and below you, than that you were at the bottom of the sea. In a dead calm you could see the sun; it looked like a purple flower, out of whose cup all the light was streaming.

Each of the young Princesses had her little plot in the garden, where she could dig and plant as she liked. One would make her flower-bed in the shape of a whale, another preferred to have hers like a little **mermaid**, but the youngest made hers quite round, like the sun, and would only have flowers that shone red like it. She **was an odd child, quiet** and thoughtful, and whereas the other sisters would deck out their gardens with the quaintest things that they had got from sunken ships, she would only have—besides the rose-red flowers that were like the sun far up in the sky—a pretty statue of marble. It **was** of a handsome boy, carved out of bright white stone, which had come down to the sea bottom from a wreck. Beside the statue she planted **a** rose-red weeping willow, which grew splendidly and hung its fresh branches over it, right down to the blue sand bottom.

on which the shadows showed violet and moved with the branches; it looked as if the top and the roots of the tree were playing at kissing each other.

She had no greater delight than in dreaming about the world of men up above. The old grandmother had to tell her all she knew about ships and horses and men and animals. It seemed to her particularly delightful that up there on earth the flowers smelt sweet (which they did not at the sea-bottom) and that the woods were green and the fish which one saw among the branches could sing so loud and prettily that it was a joy to hear them. It was the little birds that the grandmother called fish, otherwise they would not have understood, for they had never seen a bird.

"When you're full fifteen years old," said the grandmother, "you shall have leave to come up out of the sea and sit on the rocks in the moonlight, and see the big ships that come sailing by; and forests and houses you shall see."

During the year that was passing one of the sisters was fifteen years old; but the rest— why, each was one year younger than the next, and so the youngest had a clear five years to wait before she could come up from the sea bottom and see how things go with us. But the first promised the next one to tell her what **she** had seen and had thought beautiful on the first day, for their grandmother **didn't** tell them enough: there were very many things they **wanted** to know about.

None of them was so full of longing as the youngest, the very one who had the longest time to wait, and was so quiet and thoughtful. Many a night she s___d at the open window and gazed up throug___ ___ dark blue waters wher___ the fish went ___ their **fins and tails**. She could see th___ ___ the stars; of course they were ve___ ___en through the water, they lo___ ___ than they do to our eyes. If ___ ___ack cloud passed along ben___ ___ew that it was ei___ ___ve her, or even ___ ___e in it. Certai___ ___eneath them ___ ___ stretching ___ ___e eldest ___ ___as fifteen ___ and could rise ___ ___ surface of the sea.

When she came back ___ ___ndred

5

...to tell you...the most beautiful thing, she said, was to lie on a sandbank in the moonlight in the calm sea, and to see close by the shore the big town where the lights twin- kled like hundreds of stars, and to hear the sound of music and the noise and stir of carts **and** people, and see all the church towers and steeples, and hear the bells ringing; and just because she could not get up there, she **longed** after all that most of all.

Oh, how the youngest sister did listen! And when, later on in the evening, she stood at the open window and gazed up through the dark blue water, she thought about the big town and all the noise and stir, and there she fancied she could hear the church bells ring- ing down to her.

The year after, the second sister had leave **to rise up through the water** and swim where she liked; she ducked up just as the sun was going down, and the sight of that she thought the most beautiful sight in the whole wide world. The sky around had looked like gold, and the clouds—ah, the beauty of them she could never describe; red and violet, they sailed past above her; but far swifter than they, there flew a large white veil, a great flock of wild

6

s away over the water, to where the sun
wa. She swam to it, but ... and the
rosy glow died from the clo... and the face
of the ...

Next ... the third sist... went up; she was
the boldest of them all; and so she swam u...
a broad river that ran into the sea. Beauti...
green hills she saw, with rows of vines ...
them. Palaces and mansions peeped out fro...
among stately woods. She heard all the birds
singing, and the sun shone so hot that she had
to dive beneath the water to cool her burn...
... In that water she came upon a whole
... of young human children; they were
quite naked, and ran about and splashed in
the water. She wanted to play with them, but
... away in a fright, and then came a little...
tle black creature (it was a dog, but she had
never seen a dog before) and it barked at her
so dreadfully that she was terrified and took
refuge in the open sea, but never could
forget the splendid woods, and the green hills,
and the pretty children who could swim in
the water, though they had no tails.

The fourth sister was ... She
sailed out in the lonely ... ... that was the most beautiful of all ...

7

could see many many miles all round, and the
arched over ... great bell of
... s she h... ..n, but far... way the ...
... gull... ... merry ... ...ins ... ...urned
...some... ...s, and the ... whale ... squirted
... out of their nos... ... ...at it looked
like hundreds of fountains all around her.

Now came the turn of the fifth sister. Her
birthday, it ha...ened, was in winter, and so
she saw what the others had not seen on their
first visit. The sea was all green to look at, and
round about there floated large icebergs, ev-
eryone looking like a pearl, she said, and yet
... ...bigger than ... ...owers
... men b... They ... ed themselves in
the stra...est shape... ...were like ...iamonds.
She had ...ated ...on one of ... larges...
and all the ... ...ade a ...ide circ...
away from the place where she was sitting and
letting the wind set her long hair flying; but
on towards eveni... ... wh... ...vered with
clouds, it li...... and thun...red, while
the blac... ...ed the mas...s o...ce high ...
... ...them glitter n t... fierce ligh...
Aboard of all the ships they ... ...
ther... was anxiety and fear, but she sat calmly
on her floating iceberg and watched the blue

8

flashes strike zig-zagging into the shining sea.

The first time any of the sisters came to the top of the water, each one of them was always entranced by all the new pretty sights she saw, but now that, as grown girls, they had leave to go up whenever they liked, it became quite ordinary to them, and they longed to be at home again; and after a month had passed they said that after all it was best down the bottom, and there one was so comfortable at home.

Often of an evening the five sisters would link arms together, and rise in a row over the water. They had lovely voices, more beautiful than any human beings, and when a storm was coming on, and they thought some ships might be lost, they would swim before the ships and sing most beautifully of how pretty it was at the bottom of the sea, and bade the seafarers not to be afraid of coming down there.

But they could not understand the words, they thought it was the storm; nor did they see any beautiful things there either, for when the ships sank they were drowned, and only as dead corpses did they reach the sea King's palace.

When on an evening the sisters rose like this, arm in arm, up through the sea, their little sister stayed behind quite alone, looking after them, it seemed as if she must have wept, but a mermaid has no tears, and that makes her suffer all the more.

"Oh! if only I was fifteen," she said, "I know I should become really fond of that world up there and of the people who have their homes there!"

At last she was fifteen years old.

"There now! We've got you off our hands," said the grandmother, the old widow Queen. "Come here, and let me dress you out like your other sisters"; and she put a wreath of white lilies on her hair, only every petal in the flower was a half pearl, and the old lady made eight large oysters take tight hold of the Princess's tail, to indicate her high rank.

"But it hurts so," said the little mermaid.

"Yes, one must suffer a little for smartness' sake," said the old lady.

Oh dear! She would gladly have shaken off all this finery and put away the heavy wreath. The red flowers in her garden became her much better, but she dare not change it.

"Good-bye," she said, and rose bright and

light as a bubble, up through the water. The
sun had just gone down when she lifted her
head above the sea, but all the clouds were
still glowing like gold and roses, and in the
midst of the pale red heaven the evening star
shone clear and beautiful. The air was soft
and fresh, and the sea dead calm. There lay a
great ship with three masts; only a single sail
was set, for no wind was stirring, and round
about on the rigging and on the yards sailors
were sitting. There was music and singing,
and as evening grew darker hundreds of var-
iegated lamps were lit. They looked as if the
flags of all nations were waving in the air. The
little mermaid swam straight up to the cab-
in window, and every time a wave lifted her
she could see through at the windows, clear
as mirrors, numbers of gaily dressed peo-
ple; but the handsomest of them all was the
young Prince with the big black eyes; he was
certainly not much over sixteen, and this was
his birthday, and that was why there were
these fine doings. The sailors danced on the
deck, and when the young Prince came out
there, more than a hundred rockets shot up
into the sky. They shone as bright as day, and
the little mermaid was quite frightened, and

dived down beneath the water, but soon she put up her head again, and then **it seemed as if all the stars** in the sky were falling down on her. She had never seen fireworks like that. Great suns whizzed round, splendid fire-fish darted into the blue heaven, and everything was reflected back from the bright calm sea. On the ship itself there was so much light that you could see every least rope, let alone the people. Oh! how handsome the young Prince was; he shook hands with the crew and smiled and laughed, while the music rang out into the beautiful night. It grew late, but the little mermaid could not take her eyes off the ship and the beautiful Prince. The coloured lamps **were** put out, no more rockets flew up into the sky, no more guns were let off, but deep down in the sea there was a murmur and a rumbling. Meanwhile she sat on the water and swung up and down, so that she could see into the cabin; but the ship now took a swifter pace, one sail after another was spread, the waves rose higher, great clouds came up in the dist...

...a terrib...

...the great ship ploughed with the...

...a bird over the wild sea...

piled itself into huge black mountains, as if to top the masts, but the ship dived down like a swan between the tall billows, and rose again over the heaving waters. To the little mermaid it seemed just a pleasant jaunt, but not so to the sailors. The ship creaked and cracked, the stout planks bent with the mighty blows that the sea dealt. The mast snapped in the midst as if it had been a reed, and the ship heeled over on her side, while the water rushed into her hull. Now the little mermaid saw they were in peril; she herself had to beware of the beams and broken pieces of the ship that were driven about in the sea. At one instant it was so pitch-dark that she could see nothing whatever; then, when it lightened, it was so bright that she could see everyone on board. Everyone was leaping as best he could. The young Prince she above all she looked for, and she saw him when the ship parted, sink down into the deep. For a moment she was full of joy that now he was coming down to her; but then she remembered that men could not live in the water, and that he could never come alive to her father's palace. No, die he must. So she swam in among the beams and

13

forgetting that they might have crushed her—dived deep beneath the water, and rose high among the billows, and so came at last to the young Prince, who could hardly keep himself afloat any longer in the stormy sea. His arms and legs were beginning to tire, his beautiful eyes were closing; but he would perforce have died had not the little mermaid come to him. She held his head above the water, and let the waves drive her with him whither they would.

At dawn the tempest was over; of the ship there was not a bit to be seen. The sun rose red and bright out of the water, and it seemed as if thereat life came into the Prince's cheeks; but his eyes were still closed. The mermaid kissed his fair high forehead and stroked back his wet hair. She thought he resembled the marble statue down in her little garden. She kissed him again and wished that he might live after all.

And now she saw in front of her the dry land, high blue hills on whose tops the white snow shone as if swans were lying there. Down front of them lay a church or an abbey (she knew not what), but at least a building. Lemon and apple trees grew in the garden, and

14

before the gate were tall palms. At this spot
the sea made a little bay; it was dead calm, but
very deep right up to the rocks where the fine
white sand was washed up. Hither she swam
with the fair Prince and laid him on the sand,
but took care that his head should rest upper-
most in the warm sunshine.

Now the bells rang out from the great
white building, and a number of young
maidens came out through the gardens. The
little mermaid swam farther out, behind
some high boulders which stuck up out of
the water, laid some sea foam over her hair
and her bosom, so that no one could see
her little face, and there she watched to see
who would come to the poor Prince. It was
not long before a young girl came that way,
and seemed to become quite terrified, but only for
a moment. Then she fetched more people,
and the mermaid saw the Prince revive, and
he smiled on all those about him, but he did
not send a smile to her, for indeed he had, of course,
no notion that she had rescued him. She felt
very sad, and when he was carried into the
great building she dived sorrowfully down
into the water and betook herself home to
her father's.

She had always been quiet and thoughtful, but now she became much more so. The sisters asked her what she had seen the first time she went up, but she did not tell them anything about it.

Every evening and morning did she go up to the place where she had left the Prince. She saw how the fruits in the garden grew ripe and were picked; she saw how the snow melted on the high mountains; but the Prince she never saw, so she always turned homeward sadder than before. It was her one comfort to sit in her little garden and throw her arms about the fair marble statue which was like the Prince; but she took no care of her flowers, and they spread as in a wild wood over all the paths, and wove their long stems and leaves in among the branches of the trees, so that it was quite dark there.

At last she could contain herself no longer, but told one of her sisters, and at once all the others got to know it, but nobody else except them and just one or two other mermaids who didn't tell anyone but their dearest friends. One of these could tell who the Prince was; she too had seen the fete on the ship, and knew where he came from and

16

where his kingdom lay.

"Come, little sister," said the others cesses, and with their arms about each other shoulders they rose in a long line out of the sea in front of the spot where they knew the Prince's palace was.

It was built of a kind of pale yellow shining stone, with great marble steps that you could go down straight into the sea. Stately gilded domes rose above the roof, and between the pillars that surrounded the whole building stood statues of marble which seemed alive. Through the clear glass of the tall windows you could see into the noble halls, where costly silk curtains and tapestries were hung, and all the walls were decked with great paintings that it was delightful to gaze at. In the middle of the largest hall a great fountain splashed; its jet soared high up towards the glass dome in the roof, through which the sun shone on the water and on the beautiful plants that grew in the wide basin.

Now she knew where he lived, and thither she came on many an evening and night upon the water. She swam much closer to the land than any of the others had dared to do; she even went right up the narrow canal ben the stately balcony of marble, which cast a shadow far over the water. Here she would sit and gaze at the young Prince, who believed himself to be quite alone in the bright moon-light.

Many an evening she saw him sail, to the sound of music, in his splendid boat, where the flags waved; she peeped out from among the green weed, and if the breeze caught her long silver white veil, and anyone saw it, they thought it was a swan flapping its wings.

Many a night when the fishermen lay out at sea with torches, she heard them telling all manner of good about the young Prince, and it made her glad that she had saved his life when he was being tossed half dead upon the waves, and she thought of how close his head had lain on her bosom, and how loving-ly she had kissed him then; he knew nothing whatever about it, and could not so much as dream about her.

She became fonder and fonder of human people, and more and more did she long to be able to go up amongst them. Their world, she thought, was far larger than hers: for they could fly far over the sea in ships, climb high up above the clouds on the lofty mountains.

and the lands they owne[d] [...]
forests and fields farther than [...] [s]ee.
There was a great deal she wanted t[o] [kn]ow, but
her sisters could not answer all her questions,
so she asked the old grandmother: she knew
well the upper world, as she very properly
calle[d] [...] [ab]ove the sea.

[...] [peo]ple aren't drowned,"
the [...] [aske]d, "can they go on
livi[ng] [...] [the]y die as we do down
here in [...]

"Yes," sa[id] [th]e old lady, "they have to die,
too, and be[sides] their lifetime is shorter than
ours. We can live for three hundred [...]
when we cease to be here, we o[nly] [...]
foam on the water, and have not e[ven] [...]
down here among our dear ones. [...]
no immortal [soul, w]e never live again, [...]
are like [...] [on]ce it is cut down
it n[...] [hu]man kind, on
th[...] [h]ave a s[oul that] lives always
[...] [e]arth. It rises
[...] [cl]ear air, [...] the shining
[...] [r]ise [...] [se]a and look at
[...] [peo]ple's [...] so do they rise
[...] beautiful places, which we

19

"Why did we have no immortal souls given us?" said the little mermaid, very sadly. "I would give all my hundreds of years that I have to live to be a human being for only one day, and then get a share in the heavenly world."

"You mustn't go thinking about that," said the old lady, "we have a much happier and better lot than the people up there."

"So then I've got to die and float like foam on the sea and not hear the noise of the waves, and see the lovely flowers and the red sun! Can't I do anything at all to gain an everlasting soul?"

"No," said the old lady, "only if a human being held you so dear that you were to him more than father or mother, and if with all his thoughts and affections he clung to you and made the priest lay his right hand in yours with the promise to be faithful to you here and for ever, then his soul would flow over into your body, and you too would have a share in the destiny of men. He would give you a soul and still keep his own. But that can never happen. The very thing that is counted beautiful here in the sea, I mean your fish's tail, they think horrid up there on the earth;

20

they have no notion of what's proper; up there people must needs have two clumsy props which they call legs, in order to look nice."

The little mermaid sighed and looked sadly at her fish's tail. "Let's be cheerful," said the old lady. "We'll jump and dance about for the three hundred years we have to live. It's long enough in all conscience; after that one can sleep it out all the pleasanter in one's grave. ...ight... ...to have a court ball."

Truly, it was a magnificent affair, such as ...n earth. The walls and ceiling of the great ballroom were of glass, thick but clear. Many hundreds of large mussel-shells, rose-red and grass-green, were set in rows on either side, with a blue flame burning in them that lighted up the whole hall and shone out through the walls, so that the sea outside was all lit up. You could see all the innumerable fish, big and little, swimming round the glass walls. The scales of some of them shone purple-red, on others they shone like silver and gold. In the middle of the hall there flowed a broad rapid stream, and on it the men and mermaids danced to their own beautiful singing. Such charming voices no one on earth possesses. The little mermaid sang the most

she knew that

she did not,

like

love

him

Her
heart beat with terror, and she almost turned
back,   she thought of the Prince

she

...through the water, in among the terri-
ble polypi which stretched out their
arms and fingers after her. She saw that ev-
eryone of these held something it had caught,
hundreds of little arms held it like strong
hands of iron. Men who had been lost at sea
and had sunk deep down there, looked out,
white skeletons, from among the arms of the
polypi. Rudders of ships and chests they held,
and skeletons of land beasts, and even a little
mermaid, which they had caught and killed.
That, to her, was almost the most frightful
thing of all.

Now she came to a great slimy clearing
in the wood, where large fat water-snakes
wallowed, showing their ugly whitey-yel-
low coils. In the centre of the clearing was a
house built of the white bones of men: there
the Sea Witch sat, making a toad feed out of
her mouth, as we make a little canary bird eat
sugar.

The hideous fat water-snakes she called
her little chickens, and let them roll out over
her great spongy bosom.

"I know well enough what you want," said
the Sea Witch, "and a silly thing, too: all the
same, you shall have your way, for..."

you to a bad end, my pretty Prin... you
want to be rid of your... tail an...
props to walk o... ...ad, like h...
the young ... ...lov... ...u
and you n... ...immortal soul.
With that th... ...aug... so loud and so
hideously that t... ...d and th...
bled down on to the g... and wallowed
... You've ... in th...ick o...
time," said the Wit... ...ter sun-
rise I couldn't help yo... ...r came
round. I shall make a dri... ...you, and with
... ...before the sun
rises, put yourself on the b...
...t and open
into what men call pretty leg... ...
it'll be li... ...p sword going through you.
Everybody t...t sees you will say you are the
prettiest human child they ... ...
keep your swimming ga... ...dancer wi...
...float along like you. But every step
...treading on
a sharp knife, so th... ...would think your
blood must gush out... you ca... ...nat,
I will do what you wish."

"Yes," said the little mermaid, with a fal-
tering voice; and she thought of the Prince

...winning an immortal soul. "But re-
...said the witch, "when you've once
...ken a human shape, ...ever be...me
...a mermaid again, ...ca...
through the water to your sister...
father's palace; and if you...
of the Pri...so th...
ther and mo...
his thoughts, and mak...e priest...
hands in one another's, so th...
...wife, then you wo......you...
...first mo...ng after he...
...e, your heart will br...
...and...foam...the...
...said the...mermaid,
...corpse.

...t I must be paid, too," said th...
...it's not a small matter that...
the loveliest voice of...
...bottom of the se...
... you'll...

...cio...my own
blood in it, th......may be as sharp as
...edged sword.
...but if you take away my voice," said the
...mermaid, "what have I left?"

26

"Your beautiful form," said the witch, "and your floating gait, and your speaking eyes: with them you can easily delude a human heart. What, have you lost courage? Put out your little tongue, and I'll cut it off for the fee, and you shall have the potent drink."

"Yes," said the little mermaid, and the witch put the cauldron on the fire to brew the drink. "Cleanliness is a good thing," said she, and scoured the cauldron with snakes which she tied up in a knot. Then she scratched her breast and let the black blood drop into the pot. The steam took dreadful shapes, enough to fill one with fear and horror. Every moment the witch threw something afresh into the cauldron, and when it was really boiling, the sound was like that of a crocodile weeping. At last the drink was ready, and it looked like the clearest of water.

"There you are," said the witch, and cut off the tongue of the little mermaid. Now she was dumb, she could neither sing nor speak.

"If the polypi should catch you when you are going back through my wood," said the Witch, "just throw one drop of this drink on them, and their arms and fingers will burst into a thousand bits." But there was no need

the little mermaid **to** do that; the poly-
p... shrank back in fear before her when they
saw the shining drink which glittered in her
hand as if it had been a twinkling star. So she
passed quickly through the wood, and the
marsh, and the roaring maelstrom.

... could ... her father's palace. The
t... the ... quenched in the great ballroom.
... no doubt every one in there was asleep, but
she **dared** not go to them now that she was
dumb and was going to leave them **for** ever.
It seemed as if her heart must burst asun-
der with sorrow. She stole into the garden
and took one flower from each of her sister's
flower beds, and blew on her fingers a thou-
sand kisses towards the palace, and rose up
through the dark blue sea.

The sun was not yet up when she saw the
Prince's palace, and clambered up the stately
marble steps. The moon was shining beauti-
fully bright. The little mermaid swallowed the
sharp burning drink, and it was as though a
two-edged sword was piercing her **delicate**
body: she swooned with the pain, and lay as
one dead. When the sun shone out over the
sea, she awoke and felt a torturing pang, but
right in front of her stood the beautiful young

28

Prince. He fixed his coal-black ___ on her, so that she cast her own eyes down, and s__ __at her fish's tail was gone and that she n__ __d the prettiest small white **legs** that __ny young girl could have. But she was quite naked, so she wrapped he__ __ mass__ __ long hair. **The** Pri__ __ was and how she had c__ __azed at him **sweet**ly and y__ __k blue eyes, for she could no__ __p __ __ took her by the hand and __ h__ __ __he palace. Every step she too__ __as, __ __ __ **witch** had warned her, as if s__e __as tr__ __g on pointed swords and shar__ k__ve__ __e__ __e bore it gladly. Led by the Prin__es __a__ __he walked light as a bubble, __nd __he a__ __veryone else marv__ll__d at her graceful l__ __ __g__ it.

Cost__y ro__e __f __lk a__d muslin we__ upon her, a__d sh__ wa__ th__ __ __f __ palace; but she __w__s d__m__ __ __ speak nor sing. __ea__tiful sl__ __s __ silks and gol__ **came forward** __ __ang to t__ Prince and his ro__al parents. __ __e sang more sweetly than all the rest, and __he Prince applauded her **and smiled** on her. Then the little mermaid was sad, for she knew that she herself had sung far more sweetly; and she thought: Oh! if he could but know that to be near him I have given my voice away for ever!

Then the slave girls danced graceful floating dances to the noblest of music, and now the little mermaid raised her pretty white arms and rose on tip-toe and floated over the floor, and danced as none had ever yet danced. At every movement her beauty grew yet more on the sight, and her eyes spoke more deeply to the heart than the song of the slave girls.

Everyone was enraptured by it, and more than all, the Prince, who called her his little foundling; and she danced again and again, though every time her foot touched the ground it was as though she was treading on sharp knives. The Prince said that now she should always be near him, and she was allowed to sleep outside his door on a cushion of silk.

He had a boy's dress made for her, so that she might ride with him on horseback. They rode through the sweet-smelling woods, where the green boughs brushed her shoulders, and the little birds sang in the cover of the young leaves. With him she clambered up the high mountains, too; though her delicate feet were cut so that everyone could see, she only laughed, and followed him till they could see the clouds beneath them like a flock of birds flying towards the distant lands.

At home at the Prince's palace, when at night all the others were asleep, she would go out to the broad marble stairs, and it cooled her burning feet to stand in the cold sea water, and then she thought about those who were down in the deeps below.

One night her sisters came up arm in arm, singing mournfully as they swam on the water, and she beckoned to them, and they recognized her, and told her how sad she had made them all. After that they visited her every night; and one night she saw far out in the sea, the old grandmother, who had not been to the top of the water for many a year, and the Sea King, with his crown on his head. They stretched their arms towards her, but they dared not trust themselves so near the land as the sisters.

Day by day she grew dearer to the Prince: he loved her as one might love a dear good child, but he never had a thought of making her his Queen: and his wife she must be, or else she could never win an immortal soul, but on his wedding morning she would turn into foam on the sea.

"Are not you fonder of me than of all the rest?" the little mermaid's eyes **seemed** to say when he took her in his arms and kissed her fair brow. "Yes, you are dearest of all to me," said the Prince, "for you have the best heart of them all. You are dearest to me, and you are like a young maiden whom I saw once and certainly shall never meet again. I was on a ship that was wrecked, and the waves drove me to land near a holy temple **where** a number of young maidens ministered. The youngest of them found me on the bank and saved my life. I saw her only twice. She was the only one I could love in all the world, but you are like her, you almost stamp her likeness on my soul. She belongs to that holy temple, and therefore my good fortune has sent you to me, and we never will part." "Ah, he doesn't know that I saved his life," thought the little mermaid. "I bore him over the sea, away to the grove where the temple stands; I sat behind him in the foam and watched to see if anyone would come, and saw the pretty maiden whom he loves more than me"; and the mermaid heaved a deep sigh. Weep **she** could not: "'The maiden **belongs** to the holy temple," he said; she will never come out into the world: they will never meet again. I am with him, I see him every day. I will tend him and love him and give up my life to him."

But now the Prince was to be married, people said, and to take the beautiful daughter of the neighbouring king; and it was for that that he was fitting out such a splendid ship. "They say, of course, that the Prince is going to travel to see the country of the king next door, but it really is to see his daughter. He's to have a great suite with him." But the little mermaid shook her head and laughed; she knew the Prince's mind better than anyone else. "I must travel," he had said to her, "I must see the pretty Princess; my father and mother require that, but they will not force me to bring her home as my bride. I cannot love her. She is not like the fair maiden of the temple, as you are. If ever I chose a bride it would be you, my first, my dumb foundling with the speaking eyes." And he kissed her red lips and played with her long hair and laid his head on her heart, so that it dreamed of man's destiny and an undying soul.

"You're not afraid of the sea, are you, my dumb child?" he said, as they stood on the splendid ship that was to bear them to the country of the neighbouring King. And he told her of storms and calm, of strange **fishes** in the deep, and of what divers had seen down there, and she smiled at his description, for, **of course,** she knew more than anybody else about the bottom of the sea. In the moonlit night, when all but the steersman were asleep, she sat on the gunwale of the ship and gazed down through the clear water and fancied she saw her father's palace. On the summit of it stood the old grandmother, with **a** crown of silver on her head, gazing up through the swift current at the ship's keel. Then her sisters came up upon the water, and looked mournfully at her and wrung their white hands. She beckoned to them and smiled, and wanted to tell them that all was going well and happily with her, but then the ship's **boy** came towards her, and the sisters dived down; so he thought the white arms he had seen were foam on the

morning the ship sailed into the neighbouring King's fine city. out, and from the blaring of trumpets, paraded with waving flags and glittering bayonets. [...] a fete, balls and parties fo[...] other; but as yet the Prince [...] n[...] She was being brought up fa[...] in a s[...] temple, they said, and there [...]s learning all royal accomplishments. At la[...] she arrived.

The little mermaid waited, eager to see her beauty, and she had to confess that a more graceful form she had **never** seen. The skin was so delicate and pure, and behind the long dark eyelashes a pair of dark-blue beautiful eyes smiled out.

"It is you!" said the Prince, "you, who saved me when I lay like a corpse on the shore!" and he clasped his blushing bride in his arms. "Oh, I am more than happy!" he said to the little mermaid; "my dearest wish, the thing I never dared hope for, has been granted me. You will rejoice in my happiness, for you are fonder of me than all the rest," and the little mermaid kissed his hand, and thought she felt her heart breaking. His wedding morning would bring death to her, and **would change her** [...] nto foam upon the sea.

All the church bells were ringing; the heralds rode about and proclaimed the betrothal. On every altar fragrant oil was burning in precious silver lamps; the priests swung their censers, and the bride and bridegroom joined hands and received the blessing of the Bishop. The little mermaid, clad in silk and gold, stood holding the bride's train; but her ears heard not the festal music, her eyes saw not the holy rite; she thought on the eve of her death of all that she had lost in the world.

That very evening the bride and the bridegroom embarked on the ship, and the cannons were fired and the flags waved, and amidship was raised a royal tent of gold and purple with the loveliest of curtains, and there the married pair were to sleep in that calm cool night.

The sails bellied in the wind, and the ship glided easily and with little motion, away over the bright sea.

When it grew dark, variegated lamps were lit and the crowd danced merry dances on the deck. The little mermaid could not but think of the first time she rose up out of the sea and saw that same splendour and merriment; and she too whirled about in the dance, swerving as the swallow swerves when it is chased; and everyone was in ecstasies of wonder at her: never before had she danced so wonderfully.

Sharp knives seemed to be cutting her deli-
cate feet, but **she** hardly **felt** it the wounds in
her heart were sharper. She knew that was the
last night she woul see hi for whom she
had forsaken her ra e and h r h me, and giv-
en up her l ve you , an da y had suffered
unending pa n h kr ow o him. This was the
last night th sh w ld breathe the same air
as he, o ee he eep **ocean** and the starlit
heav. e et o i t without thought,
without dre er wh neither had
a sou or

t al ent aboard
the hip laughed
and a **in her**
heart. The tiful brid
nd he play ir, d a n
in m we he en d t.
    It was still and qu ne on he s only
the helmsman st d a h til el e
mer naid l d h v ite a s ub
and e ed stw d rth red d n he
ay o u sun, e ne wo d l er.
Then e sa he ste s ri o of e sea;
they w le ass th ir t ti il ng hair
no longe h d t el ez had been
cut off.

"We ha[...] [...]h to make her help us [...] die to-night. She has giv[...] [...] it is! Do you see how sha[...] [...] e sun rises you must plunge [...] [...]ce's heart, and when his w[...] [...]es out upon your feet, they [...] [...]er into a fish tail and you w[...] [...]ermaid again, and will be a[...] [...]n to us in the water and [...] [...]red years before [...] [...]am. Make [...] [...] [...] [...] [...] [...] [...] [...] [...] [...] [...] [...] [...] [...] [...] sky, and [...] [...]t die a[...] with a strange heavy [...] they sank be-[...]th the waves.

The little mermaid drew aside the purple [cu]rtain of the tent and saw the beautiful bride sleeping with her head on the Prince's breast, and she stopped and kissed him on his fair brow, and looked at the sky where the red of the dawn was shining brighter and brighter, looked at the sharp knife, and fixed her eyes

38

again on the Prince, who in his sleep was murmuring the name of his bride. She alone was in his thoughts, and the knife quivered in the mermaid's hand—but then—she cast it far out into the waves, and where it fell they shone red, and it seemed as if drops of blood spurted up out of the water. Once more she gazed with a half-dying glance on the Prince, and then threw herself from the ship into the sea, and felt that her body was dissolving into foam.

Now the sun ascended out of the sea, and his rays fell mild and warm upon the death-cold foam, and the little mermaid felt no touch of death. She saw the bright sun, and above her floated hundreds of lovely transparent forms. Through them she could see the white sails of the ship and the rosy clouds in the sky. Their voices were as music, but so ethereal that no human ear could hear it, just as no earthly eye could see them: wingless, they floated by their own lightness through the air. The little mermaid saw that she too had a body like theirs, which was rising further and further up out of the foam.

"To whom am I coming?" said she, and her voice rang like that of the other beings, so ethereally, that no earthly music can re-echo

"To the daughters of the air" the others answered; "the mermaid has no immortal soul
and can never gain one unless she wins the
love of a mortal, for on the power outside her
that her eternal being depends. The daughters
of the air have no everlasting soul either, but
they can by good deeds shape one for themselves. We are flying to the hot countries,
where the stagnant air of pestilence kills men;
there we waft coolness, we spread the perfume
of the flowers through the air and send men
new life and healing. When for three hundred
years we have striven to do the good we can,
we receive an immortal soul and have a share
in the everlasting happiness of mankind. You,
poor little mermaid, have striven for that too
with all your heart, you have suffered and endured and raised yourself into the world of the
spirits of the air, and you also, by good deeds,
can shape for yourself an immortal soul in the
space of three hundred years."

And the little mermaid raised her bright
arms towards God's sun, and for the first time
she felt the gift of tears.

On the ship there was stir and life again.

in deep sorrow they gazed down into

the bride's forehead, and on him she smiled

sailing

we shall float i

don and we may reach it yet sooner," whis-

of them. "Unseen we float into th

on which we find a good child th

makes love

our time of trial. The ch

not know en we are flying thr

is taken the three

we see a perverse d evil chi

weep in sorrow, and very te we shed adds

MERMAID
(Or, How to Find Love Underwater)

the little mermaid was an odd child, quiet
as a violet in the moonlight.
she didn't want her fins and tail
and longed to rise up through the water
to where the sun was, forget
the green glitter of the zigzagging sea.
to leave the ordinary and be a human being.
she was fifteen. goodbye she said, bright as gold.
the sea was stirring, evening grew
hundreds of black eyes in the sky,
it seemed as if all the stars were broken.
at one instant she saw him in the water,
the prince, who could hardly keep himself afloat.
the sun rose red as an apple as she swam
with the prince and laid him on the sand.
of course she rescued him.
she had always been thoughtful.
and wild with delight dared
to kiss him not very properly.
but truly, she knew she did not, like
love him. her heart beat with terror, and she almost turned
back. she thought of the prince she held like a caught little fish.
keep swimming, said the little mermaid with the loveliest
courage, at last ready to dare for delicate legs.
the sweet witch came forward and smiled,
and then beckoned her to see where she belongs.
princess of fishes, of course a boy never would change her.
the little mermaid lit up and whirled in wonder.
she felt the unending ocean in her heart,
and then her fish tail was shining brighter and brighter.
her body was music, rising like power,
and the little mermaid for the first time was
in love.

AUTHOR'S NOTE

Once upon a time, I was a fish. A Julafish. My mother gave me the nickname, and it immediately glittered and fit. During my summers I spent hours in the weightless water, imagining the tiny hydrogens and oxygens carrying me on their molecular backs. I was usually the last one to climb out of the deep end of the pool, my fingers pruney and puckered, the ends of my hair bright white from the green-chlorine, my eyes stinging, stomach singing—badges my body carried with intense pride.

Even as I grew older, the water continued to call to me. Something about swimming and summer brings me right back to being a teenager. That specific contradiction of a girl in between two worlds, wanting to feel safe and protected, but also untethered and free; wanting to stay young, but so impatient to be and seem older. I held this tension so indefinitely when I was confined by the concrete walls of the pool, but also feeling so liquidy and unloosened, my hair spreading underwater as if in slow motion, like an undiscovered seaflower. Swimming filled me with an ache and anticipation, something like purpose or maybe a promise—that something (or someone) amazing just had to come.

So perhaps it's no surprise that the story of "The Little Mermaid" always spoke deeply to me. I admired the feistiness of the kind of girl I wanted to be. Finally, this brave and rebellious explorer knew just what I was feeling. This little mermaid, full of huge longing, just like my unsinkable heart—we were two girl-fishes waiting for our real lives to begin.

But I was surprised when I reread the original Hans Christian Andersen version. Not only is this story incredibly dark and strange, I noticed things about the Little Mermaid that I had somehow ignored or dismissed. This prince-obsessed fish was willing to give away her voice, her most precious gift, just to land a boy. She was willing to change her body in exchange for someone she barely knew, who—more tragically—didn't know her, too. (And he was a terrible swimmer!)

So now, years later, it's finally my turn to tell the version of "The Little Mermaid" that I want to. Armed with my trusty permanent marker, I'm ready to rescue this story and give it back to a very specific reader—the hopeful girl I once was. The girl who identified so recklessly with the voiceless Little Mermaid. This dangerously "little" version of what girls are taught to want or expect. The girl who didn't yet know she needed a better, stronger (and yes, feminist) story. A story that also celebrates body positivity—where the water's surface is a mirror and you are grateful for the reflection you see.

And now it's my privilege to pass this revision onto you, too. To challenge you to grab a marker and pick up your own book, or, simply, turn this book over (only if you own it!) and find your own poem in the original story. To reimagine and radically change it. To find something exciting about blackout poetry and transformation, both on and off the page. I hope you engage with erasure as an act of rebellion and resistance, a poetic and sometimes destructive way to create. Take back or blackout or bury a dead story that no longer speaks to you, whose heart no longer beats for you. Uncover and choose new words and worlds that feel destined for you. Dive into your deepest desires. Erase whatever (or whoever) isn't worthy of you. Swim toward an unexpected ending—the one with the love you really wanted. The love you always deserved.

FIN

J.M. FARKAS is a poet. Erasurist. Former high school English teacher. Dental school dropout. Epic high-five-r. Scrabble enthusiast. Never-lost-a-hula-hoop-contest-ist. Her other blackout poetry books include *Be Brave* and *How to Be a Poet*. She lives in New York.

GINA TRIPLETT is a fine artist and illustrator whose work has graced everything from murals to National Award-winning novelists' books, Converse sneakers, Whole Foods brand staples, and pandemic soup cans. She lives and works in Philadelphia.

THE LITTLE
MERMAID

This version of "The Little Mermaid,"
by Hans Christian Andersen,
translated by M. R. James,
was originally published in *Forty-Two Stories*,
by Faber & Faber Ltd., London (1930).

THE LITTLE MERMAID

by
HANS CHRISTIAN ANDERSEN

cameron kids

Far out in the sea the water is as blue as the petals of the loveliest of cornflowers, and as clear as the clearest glass; but it is very deep, deeper than any anchor-cable can reach, and many church towers would have to be put one on the top of another to reach from the bottom out of the water. Down there live the sea people.

Now you must not think for a moment that there is only a bare white sandy bottom there; no, no: there the most extraordinary trees and plants grow, which have stems and leaves so supple that they stir at the slightest movement of the water, as if they were alive. All the fish, big and little, flit among the branches, like the birds in the air up here. In the deepest place of all lies the sea king's palace. The walls are of coral, and the tall pointed windows of the clearest possible amber, but the roof is of mussel-shells that open and shut themselves as the water moves. It all looks beautiful, for in everyone of them lie shining pearls, a single one of which would be the principal ornament in a Queen's crown.

The sea King down there had been a widower for many years, but his old mother kept house for him. She was a clever woman, but

proud of her rank, for which reason she went about with twelve oysters on her tail, while the rest of the nobility might only carry six. For the rest she deserved high praise, especially because she was so fond of the little sea Princesses, her grandchildren. There were six of them, beautiful children, but the youngest was the prettiest of them all. Her skin was as bright and pure as a rose-leaf, her eyes were as blue as the deepest lake; but like all the rest, she had no feet—her body ended in a fish's tail. All the love-long day they might play down in the palace in the great halls where live flowers grew out of the walls. The big windows of amber stood open, and the fishes swam in through them, just as with us swallows fly in when we open the windows; but the fishes used to swim right up to the little Princesses and feed out of their hands and allow themselves to be stroked.

Outside the palace there was a large garden with fiery red and dark blue trees, whose fruit shone like gold, and their flowers were like a flaming fire, because they were always moving their stems and leaves. The ground was of the finest sand, but blue like the flame of sulphur. Over the whole expanse down

there lay a wonderful blue sheen. You could more easily imagine that you were far up in the air and could see the sky above you and below you, than that you were at the bottom of the sea. In a dead calm you could see the sun: it looked like a purple flower out of whose cup all the light was streaming.

Each of the young Princesses had her little plot in the garden, where she could dig and plant as she liked. One would make her flower-bed in the shape of a whale, another preferred to have hers like a little mermaid, but the youngest made hers quite round, like the sun, and would only have flowers that shone red like it. She was an odd child, quiet and thoughtful, and whereas the other sisters would deck out their gardens with the quaintest things, that they had got from sunken ships, she would only have—besides the rose-red flowers that were like the sun far up in the sky—a pretty statue of marble. It was of a handsome boy, carved out of bright white stone, which had come down to the sea bottom from a wreck. Beside the statue she planted a rose-red weeping willow, which grew splendidly and hung its fresh branches over it, right down to the blue sand bottom,

on which the shadows showed violet, and moved with the branches; it looked as if the top and the roots of the tree were playing at kissing each other.

She had no greater delight than in dreaming about the world of men up above. The old grandmother had to tell her all she knew about ships and horses and men and animals. It seemed to her particularly delightful that up there on earth the flowers smelt sweet (which they did not at the sea bottom), and that the woods were green and the fish which one saw among the branches could sing so loud and prettily that it was a joy to hear them. It was the little birds that the grandmother called fish, otherwise they could not have understood, for they had never seen a bird.

"When you're full fifteen years old," said the grandmother, "you shall have leave to come up out of the sea and sit on the rocks in the moonlight, and see the big ships that come sailing by; and forests and houses you shall see."

During the year that was passing one of the sisters was fifteen years old; but the rest— why, each was a year younger than the next, and so the youngest had a clear five years to

wait before she could come up from the sea bottom and see how things go with us. But the first promised the next one to tell her what she had seen and had thought beautiful on the first day, for their grandmother didn't tell them enough: there were very many things they wanted to know about.

None of them was so full of longing as the youngest, the very one who had the longest time to wait, and was so quiet and thoughtful. Many a night she stood at the open window and gazed up through the dark blue waters where the fish went waving their fins and tails. She could see the moon and the stars; of course they were very pale, but, seen through the water, they looked much larger than they do to our eyes. If something like a black cloud passed along beneath them, she knew that it was either a whale swimming above her, or even a ship with a number of people in it. Certainly they never thought that beneath them there was a lovely little mermaid stretching her hands up towards the keel.

And now the eldest Princess was fifteen years old and could rise up above the surface of the sea.

When she came back she had a hundred

things to tell; but the most beautiful thing, she said, was to lie on a sandbank in the moonlight in the calm sea, and to see close by the shore the big town where the lights twinkled like hundreds of stars, and to hear the sound of music and the noise and stir of carts and people, and see all the church towers and steeples and hear the bells ringing; and just because she couldn't go up there, she longed after all that, most of all.

Oh, how the youngest sister did listen! And when, later on in the evening, she stood at the open window and gazed up through the dark blue water, she thought about the big town and all the noise and stir, and then she fancied she could hear the church bells ringing down to her.

The year after, the second sister had leave to rise up through the water and swim where she liked; she ducked up just as the sun was going down, and the sight of that she thought the most beautiful of all. The whole heaven, she said, had looked like gold, and the clouds—oh! the beauty of them she could not describe: red and violet, they sailed past above her, but far swifter than they there flew, like a large white ribbon, a skein of wild

swans away over the water, to where the sun was. She swam towards it, but it sank, and the rosy glow died from the clouds and the face of the sea.

Next year the third sister went up; she was the boldest of them all; and so she swam up a broad river that ran into the sea. Beautiful green hills she saw, with rows of vines upon them. Palaces and mansions peeped out from among stately woods. She heard all the birds singing, and the sun shone so hot that she had to dive beneath the water to cool her burning face. In a little inlet she came upon a whole crowd of young human children; they were quite naked, and ran about and splashed in the water. She wanted to play with them, but they ran away in a fright, and then came a little black creature (it was a dog, but she had never seen a dog before) and it barked at her so dreadfully that she was terrified and took refuge in the open sea; but never could she forget the splendid woods and the green hills and the pretty children who could swim in the water, though they had no fish-tails.

The fourth sister was not so daring. She stayed out in the lonely sea, and told them that that was the most beautiful of all. You

could see many many miles all round, and the sky arched over you like a great bell of glass. Ships she had seen, but far away they looked like gulls. The merry dolphins had turned somersaults, and the big whales had squirted up water out of their nostrils, so that it looked like hundreds of fountains all around her.

Now came the turn of the fifth sister. Her birthday, it happened, was in winter, and so she saw what the others had not seen on their first visit. The sea was all green to look at, and round about there floated large icebergs, everyone looking like a pearl, she said, and yet they were far bigger than the church towers that men built. They showed themselves in the strangest shapes and were like diamonds. She had seated herself on one of the largest, and all the ships made a wide circle in fear, away from the place where she was sitting and letting the wind set her long hair flying; but on towards evening the sky was covered with clouds, it lightened and thundered, while the black sea lifted the masses of ice high up, and made them glitter in the fierce lightning. Aboard of all the ships they took in sail, and there was anxiety and fear, but she sat calmly on her floating iceberg and watched the blue

flashes strike zig-zagging into the shining sea.

The first time any of the sisters came to the top of the water, each one of them was always entranced by all the new pretty sights she saw, but now that, as grown girls, they had leave to go up whenever they liked, it became quite ordinary to them, and they longed to be at home again; and after a month had passed they said that after all it was far prettier down at the bottom, and there one was so comfortable at home.

On many an evening the five sisters would link arms together and rise in a row above the water. They had lovely voices, more beautiful than any human being's, and when a storm was coming on, and they thought some ships might be lost, they would swim before the ships and sing most beautifully of how pretty it was at the bottom of the sea, and bade the seafarers not to be afraid of coming down there.

But they could not understand their words; they thought it was the storm. Nor did they see any beautiful things down there either, for when the ship sank they were drowned, and only as dead corpses did they ever reach the sea King's palace.

When of an evening the sisters rose like this, arm in arm, up through the sea, their little sister was left behind quite alone, looking after them, and it seemed as if she must have wept, but a mermaid has no tears, and that makes her suffer all the more.

"Oh! if only I was fifteen," she said, "I know I shall become really fond of that world up there and of the people who have their homes there!"

At last she was fifteen years old.

"There now! We've got you off our hands," said the grandmother, the old widow Queen. "Come here, and let me dress you out like your other sisters"; and she put a wreath of white lilies on her hair, only every petal in the flower was a half-pearl, and the old lady made eight large oysters take tight hold of the Princess's tail, to indicate her high rank.

"But it hurts so," said the little mermaid.

"Yes, one must suffer a little for smartness' sake," said the old lady.

Oh dear! She would gladly have shaken off all this finery and put away the heavy wreath. The red flowers in her garden became her much better; but she dare not change it. "Good-bye," she said, and rose bright and

light as a bubble, up through the water. The sun had just gone down when she lifted her head above the sea, but all the clouds were still glowing like gold and roses, and in the midst of the pale red heaven the evening star shone clear and beautiful. The air was soft and cool, and the sea dead calm. There lay a great ship with three masts; only a single sail was set, for no wind was stirring, and round about on the rigging and on the yard, sailors were sitting. There was music and singing, and as evening grew darker hundreds of variegated lamps were lit. They looked as if the flags of all nations were waving in the air. The little mermaid swam straight up to the cabin window, and every time a wave lifted her, she could see through at the windows, clear as mirrors, numbers of gaily dressed people; but the handsomest of them all was the young Prince with the big black eyes: he was certainly not much over sixteen, and this was his birthday, and that was why there were all these fine doings. The sailors danced on the deck, and when the young Prince came out there, more than a hundred rockets shot up into the sky. They shone as bright as day, and the little mermaid was quite frightened and

dived down beneath the water, but soon she put up her head again, and then it seemed as if all the stars in the sky were falling down on her. She had never seen fireworks like that. Great suns whizzed round, splendid fire-fish darted into the blue heaven, and everything was reflected back from the bright calm sea. On the ship itself there was so much light that you could see every least rope, let alone the people. Oh! how handsome the young Prince was; he shook hands with the crew and smiled and laughed, while the music rang out into the beautiful night. It grew late, but the little mermaid could not take her eyes off the ship and the beautiful Prince. The coloured lamps were put out, no more rockets flew up into the sky, no more guns were let off, but deep down in the sea there was a murmur and a rumbling. Meanwhile she sat on the water and swung up and down, so that she could see into the cabin; but the ship now took a swifter pace, one sail after another was spread, the waves rose higher, great clouds came up in the distance, there was lightning. Oh, there would be a terrible storm; and the seamen took in sail. The great ship ploughed with the speed of a bird over the wild sea, the water

piled itself into huge black mountains, as if to top the masts, but the ship dived down like a swan between the tall billows, and rose again over the heaving waters. To the little mermaid it seemed just a pleasant jaunt, but not so to the sailors. The ship creaked and cracked, the stout planks bent with the mighty blows that the sea dealt. The mast snapped in the midst as if it had been a reed, and the ship heeled over on her side, while the water rushed into her hull. Now the little mermaid saw they were in peril; she herself had to beware of the beams and broken pieces of the ship that were driven about in the sea. At one instant it was so pitch-dark that she could see nothing whatever; then, when it lightened, it was so bright that she could see everyone on board. Everyone was leaping off as best he could. The young Prince above all she looked for, and she saw him, when the ship parted, sink down into the deep. For a moment she was full of joy that now he was coming down to her; but then she remembered that men could not live in the water, and that he could never come alive to her father's palace. No, die he must not! So she swam in among the beams and planks that drove about in the water, quite

forgetting that they might have crushed her—dived deep beneath the water, and rose high among the billows, and so came at last to the young Prince, who could hardly keep himself afloat any longer in the stormy sea. His arms and legs were beginning to tire, his beautiful eyes were closing; but he would perforce have died had not the little mermaid come to him. She held his head above the water, and let the waves drive her with him whither they would.

At dawn the tempest was over; of the ship there was not a bit to be seen. The sun rose red and bright out of the water, and it seemed as if thereat life came into the Prince's cheeks; but his eyes were still closed. The mermaid kissed his fair high forehead and stroked back his wet hair. She thought he resembled the marble statue down in her little garden. She kissed him again and wished that he might live after all.

And now she saw in front of her the dry land, high blue hills on whose top the white snow shone as if swans were lying there. Down by the shore were lovely green woods, and in front of them lay a church or an abbey (she knew not what), but at least a building. Lemon and apple trees grew in the garden, and

before the gate were tall palms. At this spot the sea made a little bay; it was dead calm, but very deep right up to the rocks where the fine white sand was washed up. Hither she swam with the fair Prince and laid him on the sand, but took care that his head should rest uppermost in the warm sunshine.

Now the bells rang out from the great white building, and a number of young maidens came out through the gardens. The little mermaid swam further out, behind some high boulders which stuck up out of the water, laid some sea-foam over her hair and her bosom, so that no one could see her little face, and there she watched to see who would come to the poor Prince. It was not long before a young girl came that way, and seemed to be quite terrified, but only for a moment. Then she fetched more people, and the mermaid saw the Prince revive, and smile on all those about him. But on her, out there, he did not smile; he had, of course, no notion that she had rescued him. She felt very sad, and when he was carried into the great building, she dived sorrowfully down into the water, and betook herself home to her father's palace.

She had always been quiet and thoughtful, but now she became much more so. The sisters asked her what she had seen the first time she went up, but she did not tell them anything about it.

Every evening and morning did she go up to the place where she had left the Prince. She saw how the fruits in the garden grew ripe and were picked; she saw how the snow melted on the high mountains; but the Prince she never saw, so she always turned homeward sadder than before. It was her one comfort to sit in her little garden and throw her arms about the fair marble statue which was like the Prince; but she took no care of her flowers, and they spread as in a wild wood over all the paths, and wove their long stems and leaves in among the branches of the trees, so that it was quite dark there.

At last she could contain herself no longer, but told one of her sisters, and at once all the others got to know it, but nobody else except them and just one or two other mermaids, who didn't tell anyone but their dearest friends. One of these could tell who the Prince was: she too had seen the fete on the ship, and knew where he came from and

where his kingdom lay.

"Come, little sister," said the other Princesses, and with their arms about each other's shoulders they rose in a long line out of the sea in front of the spot where they knew the Prince's palace was.

It was built of a kind of pale yellow shining stone, with great marble steps that you could go down straight into the sea. Stately gilded domes rose above the roof, and between the pillars that surrounded the whole building stood statues of marble which seemed alive. Through the clear glass of the tall windows you could see into the noble halls, where costly silk curtains and tapestries were hung, and all the walls were decked with great paintings that it was delightful to gaze at. In the middle of the largest hall a great fountain splashed; its jet soared high up towards the glass dome in the roof, through which the sun shone on the water and on the beautiful plants that grew in the wide basin.

Now she knew where he lived, and thither she came on many an evening and night upon the water. She swam much closer to the land than any of the others had dared to do; she even went right up the narrow canal beneath

the stately balcony of marble, which cast a shadow far over the water. Here she would sit and gaze at the young Prince, who believed himself to be quite alone in the bright moonlight.

Many an evening she saw him sail, to the sound of music, in his splendid boat, where the flags waved; she peeped out from among the green weed, and if the breeze caught her long silver white veil, and anyone saw it, they thought it was a swan flapping its wings.

Many a night when the fishermen lay out at sea with torches, she heard them telling all manner of good about the young Prince, and it made her glad that she had saved his life when he was being tossed half dead upon the waves, and she thought of how close his head had lain on her bosom, and how lovingly she had kissed him then; he knew nothing whatever about it, and could not so much as dream about her.

She became fonder and fonder of human people, and more and more did she long to be able to go up amongst them. Their world, she thought, was far larger than hers: for they could fly far over the sea in ships, climb high up above the clouds on the lofty mountains;

and the lands they owned stretched over forests and fields farther than she could see. There was a great deal she wanted to know, but her sisters could not answer all her questions, so she asked the old grandmother: she knew well the upper world, as she very properly called the countries above the sea.

"If the human people aren't drowned," the little mermaid inquired, "can they go on living always? Don't they die as we do down here in the sea?"

"Yes," said the old lady, "they have to die, too, and besides, their lifetime is shorter than ours. We can live for three hundred years, but when we cease to be here, we only turn to foam on the water, and have not even a grave down here among our dear ones. We have no immortal souls, we never live again; we are like the green weed: once it is cut down it never grows green again. Human kind, on the other hand, have a soul that lives always after the body has turned into earth. It rises up through the clear air, up to all the shining stars; just as we rise out of the sea and look at the human people's country, so do they rise up to unknown beautiful places, which we never attain."

"Why did we have no immortal souls given us?" said the little mermaid, very sadly. "I would give all my hundreds of years that I have to live to be a human being for only one day, and then get a share in the heavenly world."

"You mustn't go thinking about that," said the old lady, "we have a much happier and better lot than the people up there."

"So then I've got to die and float like foam on the sea, and not hear the noise of the waves and see the lovely flowers and the red sun! Can't I do anything at all to gain an everlasting soul?"

"No," said the old lady, "only if a human being held you so dear that you were to him more than father or mother, and if with all his thoughts and affections he clung to you and made the priest lay his right hand in yours with the promise to be faithful to you here and for ever, then his soul would flow over into your body, and you too would have a share in the destiny of men. He would give you a soul and still keep his own. But that can never happen. The very thing that is counted beautiful here in the sea, I mean your fish's tail, they think horrid up there on the earth;

they have no notion of what's proper: up there people must needs have two clumsy props which they call legs, if they're to look nice."

The little mermaid sighed and looked sadly at her fish's tail. "Let's be cheerful," said the old lady. "We'll jump and dance about for the three hundred years we have to live. It's long enough in all conscience; after that one can sleep it out all the pleasanter in one's grave. To-night we're to have a court ball."

Truly, it was a magnificent affair, such as you never see on earth. The walls and ceilings of the great ballroom were of glass, thick but clear. Many hundreds of large mussel-shells, rose-red and grass-green, were set in rows on either side, with a blue flame burning in them that lighted up the whole hall and shone out through the walls, so that the sea outside was all lit up. You could see all the innumerable fish, big and little, swimming round the glass walls. The scales of some of them shone purple-red, on others they shone like silver and gold. In the middle of the hall there flowed a broad rapid stream, and on it mermen and mermaids danced to their own beautiful singing. Such charming voices no one on earth possesses. The little mermaid sang the most

beautifully of them all, and they clapped their hands at her, and for a moment she felt joy at her heart, for she knew that she had the loveliest voice of anyone on earth or sea. But soon she began to think again about the world above her. She could not forget the handsome Prince, and her own sorrow that she did not, like him, possess an immortal soul. So she stole out of her father's palace, and while everything there was song and merriment she sat sadly in her little garden. There she heard the beating waves sounding down through the water, and she thought, sure, he is sailing up there, he whom I love more than father or mother, he to whom my thoughts cling and in whose hand I would lay the destiny of my life. I would risk everything to win him and an immortal soul. While my sisters are dancing in my father's palace, I will go to the old Sea Witch. I've always been dreadfully afraid of her, but it may be she can advise me and help me.

So the little mermaid went off out of her garden, towards the roaring maelstrom behind which the witch lived. She had never been that way before. No flowers grew there, and no sea grass: only the bare grey sandy

bottom stretched out round the maelstrom, where the water whirled round like a roaring millwheel and swept everything it caught hold of down with it into the deep. Right through those tearing whirls she must go to enter the Sea Witch's domain, and here for a long way the only path ran over hot bubbling mire which the Witch called her peat moss. Behind it lay her house, in the middle of a hideous wood. All the trees and bushes of it were polypi, half animal and half plant, which looked like hundred-headed snakes growing out of the ground. All their branches were long slimy arms with fingers like pliant worms, and joint after joint they kept in motion from the root till the outermost tip. Everything in the sea that they could grasp they twined themselves about, and never let it go again. The little mermaid was in terrible fear as she stopped outside the wood. Her heart beat with terror, and she almost turned back, but then she thought of the Prince and of the human soul, and so she took courage. She bound her long flowing hair close about her head, so that the polypi should not catch her by it; she joined her two hands together on her breast, and darted along as a fish

darts through the water, in among the terrible polypi, which stretched out their pliant arms and fingers after her. She saw that everyone of these held something it had caught, and hundreds of little arms held it like strong bands of iron. Men who had been lost at sea and had sunk deep down there, looked out, white skeletons, from among the arms of the polypi. Rudders of ships and chests they held fast; skeletons of land beasts, and even a little mermaid, which they had caught and killed. That, to her, was almost the most frightful thing of all.

Now she came to a great slimy clearing in the wood, where large fat water-snakes wallowed, showing their ugly whitey-yellow coils. In the centre of the clearing was a house built of the white bones of men: there the Sea Witch sat, making a toad feed out of her mouth, as we make a little canary bird eat sugar.

The hideous fat water-snakes she called her little chicks, and let them coil about over her great spongy bosom.

"I know well enough what you want," said the Sea Witch, "and a silly thing, too; all the same, you shall have your way, for it'll bring

you to a bad end, my pretty Princess. You want to be rid of your fish tail and have two props to walk on instead, like humans, so that the young Prince may fall in love with you, and you may get him and an immortal soul." With that the Witch laughed so loud and so hideously that the toad and the snakes tumbled down on to the ground and wallowed about there. "You've come just in the nick of time," said the Witch; "to-morrow after sunrise I couldn't help you till another year came round. I shall make a drink for you, and with it you must swim to the land before the sun rises, put yourself on the beach there, and drink it up; then your tail will part and open into what men call pretty legs. But it'll hurt, it'll be like a sharp sword going through you. Everybody that sees you will say you are the prettiest human child they ever saw. You'll keep your swimming gait, and no dancer will be able to float along like you. But every step you take will be as if you were treading on a sharp knife, so that you would think your blood must gush out. If you can bear all that, I will do what you wish."

"Yes," said the little mermaid, with a faltering voice; and she thought of the Prince

and of winning an immortal soul. "But remember," said the Witch, "when you've once taken a human shape, you can never become a mermaid again, you can never go down through the water to your sisters or to your father's palace; and if you don't win the love of the Prince, so that for you he forgets father and mother, and clings to you with all his thoughts, and makes the priest lay your hands in one another's, so that you become man and wife, then you won't get your immortal soul. On the first morning after he is married to anyone else, your heart will break and you will become foam on the water."

"It is my wish," said the little mermaid, pale as a corpse.

"But I must be paid, too," said the witch, "and it's not a small matter that I require. You have the loveliest voice of anyone down here at the bottom of the sea, and with it no doubt you think you'll be able to charm him; but that voice you must give me. I must have the best thing you possess as the price of my precious drink. I shall have to give you my own blood in it, that the drink may be as sharp as a two-edged sword.

"But if you take away my voice," said the

little mermaid, "what have I left?"

"Your beautiful form," said the witch, "and your floating gait, and your speaking eyes: with them you can easily delude a human heart. What, have you lost courage? Put out your little tongue, and I'll cut it off for the price, and you shall have the potent drink."

"So be it," said the little mermaid, and the witch put her cauldron on the fire to boil the magic drink. "Cleanliness is a good thing," said she, and scoured out the cauldron with some snakes which she tied in a knot. Then she scratched herself in the breast and let the black blood drip into the pot. The steam took the most dreadful shapes, enough to fill one with fear and horror. Every moment the witch cast something afresh into the cauldron, and when it was really boiling, the sound was like that of a crocodile weeping. At last the drink was ready, and it looked like the clearest of water.

"There you are," said the witch, and cut off the tongue of the little mermaid. Now she was dumb, she could neither sing nor speak.

"If the polypi should catch you when you are going back through my wood," said the Witch, "just throw one drop of that drink on

them, and their arms and fingers will break into a thousand bits." But there was no need for the little mermaid to do that; the poly-pi shrank back in fear before her when they saw the shining drink which glittered in her hand as if it had been a twinkling star. So she passed quickly through the wood, and the marsh, and the roaring maelstrom.

She could see her father's palace. The torches were quenched in the great ballroom. No doubt everyone in there was asleep, but she dared not go to them now that she was dumb and was going to leave them for ever. It seemed as if her heart must burst asunder with sorrow. She stole into the garden and took one flower from each of her sister's flower-beds, and blew on her fingers a thousand kisses towards the palace, and rose up through the dark blue sea.

The sun was not yet up when she saw the Prince's palace, and clambered up the stately marble steps. The moon was shining beautifully bright. The little mermaid swallowed the sharp burning drink, and it was as though a two-edged sword was piercing her delicate body: she swooned with the pain, and lay as one dead. When the sun shone out over the

sea, she awoke and felt a torturing pang, but right in front of her stood the beautiful young Prince. He fixed his coal-black eyes on her, so that she cast her own eyes down, and saw that her fish's tail was gone and that she now had the prettiest small white legs that any young girl could have. But she was quite naked, so she wrapped herself in her masses of long hair. The Prince asked who she was and how she had come there, and she gazed at him sweetly and yet sadly with her dark blue eyes, for she could not speak. Then he took her by the hand and led her into the palace. Every step she took was, as the witch had warned her, as if she was treading on pointed swords and sharp knives, yet she bore it gladly. Led by the Prince's hand, she walked light as a bubble, and he and everyone else marvelled at her graceful floating gait.

Costly robes of silk and muslin were put upon her, and she was the fairest of all in the palace; but she was dumb and could neither speak nor sing. Beautiful slave girls clad in silks and gold came forward and sang to the Prince and his royal parents. One sang more sweetly than all the rest, and the Prince applauded her and smiled on her. Then the lit-

tle mermaid was sad, for she knew that she herself had sung far more sweetly; and she thought: Oh! if he could but know that to be near him I have given my voice away for ever!

Then the slave girls danced graceful floating dances to the noblest of music, and now the little mermaid raised her pretty white arms and rose on tip-toe and floated over the floor, and danced as none had ever yet danced. At every movement her beauty grew yet more on the sight, and her eyes spoke more deeply to the heart than the song of the slave girls.

Everyone was enraptured by it, and more than all, the Prince, who called her his little foundling; and she danced again and again, though every time her foot touched the ground it was as though she was treading on sharp knives. The Prince said that now she should always be near him, and she was allowed to sleep outside his door on a cushion of silk.

He had a boy's dress made for her, so that she might ride with him on horseback. They rode through the sweet-smelling woods, where the green boughs brushed her shoulders, and the little birds sang in the cover of the young leaves. With the Prince she clam-

bered up the high mountains, and though her delicate feet were cut so that everyone could see, she only laughed, and followed him till they could see the clouds beneath them like a flock of birds flying towards the distant lands.

At home at the Prince's palace, when at night all the others were asleep, she would go out to the broad marble stairs, and it cooled her burning feet to stand in the cold sea water, and then she thought about those who were down in the deeps below.

One night her sisters came up arm in arm, singing mournfully as they swam on the water, and she beckoned to them, and they recognized her, and told her how sad she had made them all. After that they visited her every night; and one night she saw far out in the sea, the old grandmother, who had not been to the top of the water for many a year; and the Sea King, with his crown on his head. They stretched their arms towards her, but they dared not trust themselves so near the land as the sisters.

Day by day she grew dearer to the Prince: he loved her as one might love a dear good child, but he never had a thought of making her his Queen: and his wife she must be, or

else she could never win an immortal soul, but on his wedding morning she would turn into foam on the sea.

"Are not you fonder of me than of all the rest?" the little mermaid's eyes seemed to say when he took her in his arms and kissed her fair brow. "Yes, you are dearest of all to me," said the Prince, "for you have the best heart of them all. You are dearest to me, and you are like a young maiden whom I saw once and certainly shall never meet again. I was on a ship that was wrecked, and the waves drove me to land near a holy temple where a number of young maidens ministered. The youngest of them found me on the bank and saved my life. I saw her only twice. She was the only one I could love in all the world, but you are like her, you almost stamp her likeness on my soul. She belongs to that holy temple, and therefore my good fortune has sent you to me, and we never will part." "Ah, he doesn't know that I saved his life," thought the little mermaid. "I bore him over the sea, away to the grove where the temple stands; I sat behind him in the foam and watched to see if anyone would come, and saw the pretty maiden whom he loves more than me"; and

the mermaid heaved a deep sigh. Weep she could not: "'The maiden belongs to the holy temple,' he said; she will never come out into the world: they will never meet again. I am with him, I see him every day. I will tend him and love him and give up my life to him."

But now the Prince was to be married, people said, and to take the beautiful daughter of the neighbouring king; and it was for that that he was fitting out such a splendid ship. "They say, of course, that the Prince is going to travel to see the country of the king next door, but it really is to see his daughter. He's to have a great suite with him." But the little mermaid shook her head and laughed: she knew the Prince's mind better than anyone else. "I must travel," he had said to her, "I must see the pretty Princess; my father and mother require that, but they will not force me to bring her home as my bride. I cannot love her. She is not like the fair maiden of the temple, as you are. If ever I chose a bride it would be you first, my dumb foundling with the speaking eyes." And he kissed her red lips and played with her long hair and laid his head on her heart, so that it dreamed of man's destiny and an undying soul.

"You're not afraid of the sea, are you, my dumb child?" said he as they stood on the splendid ship that was to bear them to the country of the neighbouring King. And he told her of storms and calm, of strange fishes in the deep, and of what divers had seen down there, and she smiled at his description, for, of course, she knew more than anybody else about the bottom of the sea. In the moonlit night, when all but the steersman were asleep, she sat on the gunwale of the ship and gazed down through the clear water and fancied she saw her father's palace. On the summit of it stood the old grandmother, with a crown of silver on her head, gazing up through the swift current at the ship's keel. Then her sisters came up upon the water, and looked mournfully at her and wrung their white hands. She beckoned to them and smiled, and wanted to tell them that all was going well and happily with her; but then the ship's boy came towards her, and the sisters dived down: so he thought the white arms he had seen were foam on the sea.

Next morning the ship sailed into the harbour of the neighbouring King's fine city. All the church bells rang out, and from the

tall towers there came blaring of trumpets, while the soldiers paraded with waving flags and glittering bayonets. Every day there was a fete, balls and parties followed on one another; but as yet the Princess was not there. She was being brought up far away in a sacred temple, they said, and there was learning all royal accomplishments. At last she arrived.

The little mermaid waited, eager to see her beauty, and she had to confess that a more graceful form she had never seen. The skin was so delicate and pure, and behind the long dark eyelashes a pair of dark-blue beautiful eyes smiled out.

"It is you!" said the Prince, "you, who saved me when I lay like a corpse on the shore!" and he clasped his blushing bride in his arms. "Oh, I am more than happy!" he said to the little mermaid; "my dearest wish, the thing I never dared hope for, has been granted me. You will rejoice in my happiness, for you are fonder of me than all the rest"; and the little mermaid kissed his hand, and thought she felt her heart breaking. His wedding morning would bring death to her, and would change her into foam upon the sea.

All the church bells were ringing; the her-

alds rode about and proclaimed the betroth-al. On every altar fragrant oil was burning in precious silver lamps; the priests swung their censers, and the bride and bridegroom joined hands and received the blessing of the Bishop. The little mermaid, clad in silk and gold, stood holding the bride's train; but her ears heard not the festal music, her eyes saw not the holy rite; she thought, on the eve of her death, of all that she had lost in the world.

That very evening the bride and the bridegroom embarked on the ship, and the cannons were fired and the flags waved, and amid-ship was raised a royal tent of gold and purple with the loveliest of curtains, and there the married pair were to sleep in that calm cool night.

The sails bellied in the wind, and the ship glided easily and with little motion, away over the bright sea.

When it grew dark, variegated lamps were lit and the crew danced merry dances on the deck. The little mermaid could not but think of the first time she rose up out of the sea and saw that same splendour and merriment; and she too whirled about in the dance, swerving as the swallow swerves when it is chased; and

everyone was in ecstasies of wonder at her: never before had she danced so wonderfully. Sharp knives seemed to be cutting her delicate feet, but she hardly felt it: the wounds in her heart were sharper. She knew that was the last night she would see him for whom she had forsaken her race and her home, and given up her lovely voice, and daily had suffered unending pain unknown to him. This was the last night that she would breathe the same air as he, or see the deep ocean and the starlit heavens. An eternal night without thought, without dream, awaited her who neither had a soul nor could win one.

But all was joy and merriment aboard the ship till long past midnight. She laughed and danced with the thought of death in her heart. The Prince kissed his beautiful bride, and she played with his black hair, and arm in arm they went to rest in the splendid tent.

It was still and quiet now on the ship: only the helmsman stood at the tiller. The little mermaid laid her white arms on the bulwark and gazed eastward for the red of dawn: the first ray of the sun, she knew, would kill her. Then she saw her sisters rise out of the sea; they were pale as she, their beautiful long hair

no longer fluttered in the breeze: it had been cut off.

"We have given it to the witch to make her help us, that you may not die to-night. She has given us a knife. Here it is! Do you see how sharp it is? Before the sun rises you must plunge it into the Prince's heart, and when his warm blood gushes out upon your feet, they will grow together into a fish tail and you will become a mermaid again, and will be able to come down to us in the water and live out your three hundred years before you turn into the dead salt sea foam. Make haste! He or you must die before the sun rises. Our old grandmother has been mourning till her white hair has fallen off as ours fell before the witch's shears. Kill the Prince and come back! Make haste: do you not see the red band in the heavens? In a few minutes the sun will climb into the sky, and then you must die'; and with a strange heavy sigh they sank beneath the waves.

The little mermaid drew aside the purple curtain of the tent and saw the beautiful bride sleeping with her head on the Prince's breast, and she stopped and kissed him on his fair brow, and looked at the sky where the red of the dawn was shining brighter and brighter,

looked at the sharp knife, and fixed her eyes again on the Prince, who in his sleep was murmuring the name of his bride. She alone was in his thoughts, and the knife quivered in the mermaid's hand—but then—she cast it far out into the waves, and where it fell they shone red, and it seemed as if drops of blood spurted up out of the water. Once more she gazed with a half-dying glance on the Prince, and then threw herself from the ship into the sea, and felt that her body was dissolving into foam.

Now the sun ascended out of the sea, and his rays fell mild and warm upon the death-cold foam, and the little mermaid felt no touch of death. She saw the bright sun, and above her floated hundreds of lovely transparent forms. Through them she could see the white sails of the ship and the rosy clouds in the sky. Their voices were as music, but so ethereal that no human ear could hear it, just as no earthly eye could see them: wingless, they floated by their own lightness through the air. The little mermaid saw that she too had a body like theirs, which was rising further and further up out of the foam.

"To whom am I coming?" said she, and her voice rang like that of the other beings, so

ethereally that no earthly music can re-echo its sound.

"To the daughters of the air," the others answered; "the mermaid has no immortal soul, and can never gain one unless she wins the love of a mortal; it is on a power outside her that her eternal being depends. The daughters of the air have no everlasting soul either, but they can by good deeds shape one for themselves. We are flying to the hot countries, where the stagnant air of pestilence kills men: there we waft coolness, we spread the perfume of the flowers through the air and send men new life and healing. When for three hundred years we have striven to do the good we can, we receive an immortal soul and have a share in the everlasting happiness of mankind. You, poor little mermaid, have striven for that too with all your heart; you have suffered and endured and raised yourself into the world of the spirits of the air, and you also, by good deeds, can shape for yourself an immortal soul in the space of three hundred years."

And the little mermaid raised her bright arms towards God's sun, and for the first time she felt the gift of tears.

On the ship there was stir and life again.

She saw the Prince with his fair bride seeking for her: in deep sorrow they gazed down into the bubbling foam as if they knew she had cast herself into the waves. Unseen, she kissed the bride's forehead, and on him she smiled and then soared upward with the other children of the air to a rose-red cloud sailing in the heavens. "So, when three hundred years are over, we shall float into the heavenly kingdom, and we may reach it yet sooner," whispered one of them. "Unseen we float into the homes of men, where children are, and for every day on which we find a good child that makes its parents happy and earns their love, God shortens our time of trial. The child does not know it when we are flying through the room; and when we smile on it in happiness, a year is taken from the three hundred. But if we see a perverse and evil child, we have to weep in sorrow, and every tear we shed adds a day to our time of trial."

Hans Christian Andersen was a famous author best remembered for writing fairy tales, but likely he needed the assistance of a sly and unwavering woman.